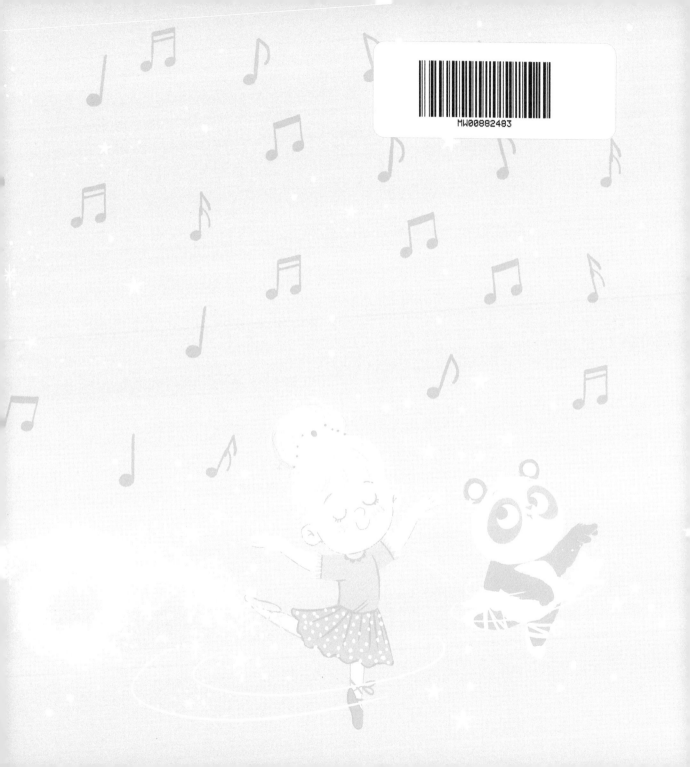

WHEN YOU ADOPT A Pandarina

For Aimee and Tom, who always keep me dancing and pick me up when I fall

—M.R.

To P.B.—Thank you for the friendship and support

—T.B.

The art in this book was created digitally.

Library of Congress Control Number 2021948104

ISBN 978-1-4197-5731-0

First published in 2021 by Hodder Children's Books, Hodder and Stoughton, London, U.K.

Text by Matilda Rose
Illustrations by Tim Budgen
Book design by Katie Messenger
Cover design by Jade Rector

Published in 2022 by Abrams Appleseed, an imprint of ABRAMS.

Printed and bound in China
10 9 8 7 6 5 4 3 2 1

For bulk discount inquiries, contact specialsales@abramsbooks.com.

ABRAMS The Art of Books
195 Broadway, New York, NY 10007
abramsbooks.com

WHEN YOU ADOPT A Pandarina

by Matilda Rose • illustrated by Tim Budgen

Abrams Appleseed
New York

Next time you're in Fairyland, make sure you visit Mrs. Paws's Haven for Magical Pets in the town of Twinkleton-Under-Beanstalk. It's truly an enchanting place. There are singing llamas, sparkly starwhals, and cuddly kitticorns.

One morning, Princess Skye arrived at the Haven for Magical Pets looking glum.

es
Haven for Magical Pets
Haven for Magical Pets
UP in the HAIR
OPEN
MAGICAL PETS INSIDE!

"How lovely to see you, Skye," said
Mrs. Paws. "But—oh dear—what's wrong?"

Skye sighed. "I'm supposed to be rehearsing
for Queen Elsie's birthday ball, but I'm no good!
When I try to dance, I trip myself up—
or even worse, one of my friends!"

Invitation

To the elegant princes and princesses
of Twinkleton Dance School:

You have been carefully selected to
perform at Queen Elsie's Birthday Ball.

Saturday, 5 p.m., Royal Twinkleton Palace

Yours sincerely,

The Palace Party Planners

Mrs. Paws smiled. "I think you need a pet to help you find your feet. Ah—I know . . .

“Skye, meet . . .

PANDARINA!”

“Pandarina LOVES to dance,” said Mrs. Paws.
“I think you two will make the perfect pair!”

As Skye skipped off
across Twinkleton Town Square,
the clock struck twelve.

"Oh dear, is that the time?"
worried Skye. "I'm going to
be late for dance class. Come
on, Pandarina, hurry!"

Skye rushed ahead,
dreaming of perfect pirouettes,
so she didn't notice Pandarina
muddling through the mud . . .

fumbling into flower beds . . .

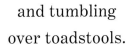

and tumbling
over toadstools.

At last they reached the
Twinkleton Dance School.

“Into position, everyone!” called Miss Twinkletoes.
Princess Skye really wanted to join in, but
as she looked around the room, she felt a
wobble of worry in her tummy.
“I think Pandarina and I will just
watch for now,” she said.

But then, as Mr. Metronome
began to play . . .

. . . Pandarina leapt onto the dance floor!

She crashed . . . and banged . . . and tumbled!

But every time Pandarina fell over, she picked herself up and kept on dancing.

Skye felt very embarrassed.

After class, Pandarina twirled, whirled, and wobbled all the way back to Sparkle Castle.

Skye felt grouchy. “You can’t get a single step right, so why do you keep trying? You’re just as clumsy as I am,” she huffed.

That night, Skye couldn't sleep. She knew she had been mean to Pandarina, but she didn't know how to make it right.

Suddenly, she heard a noise from the garden. Looking out of the window, she saw . . .

. . . Pandarina, dancing in the moonlight!

She was still a little clumsy, but each time she stumbled, she tried again with more confidence. She was slowly perfecting each move!

Princess Skye rushed outside.

"Oh, Pandarina, I'm so sorry I was unkind."

Pandarina took Skye's hand in her soft rainbow paw. As they spun around and around, Skye's worries completely disappeared. She was having **fun!**

Over the next few days, Princess Skye and Pandarina fell down a LOT.

They fell under the leafy canopy of the Enchanted Forest . . .

by the shores of Coral Cove . . .

and on the grassy plains of the Galloping Gala Fields.
But each time, they got back up and tried again. Skye's nervous thoughts faded with every twirl, skip, and jump.

At last, the day of the performance arrived. The Grand Ballroom looked magical, but as the guests cleared the dance floor, Skye's wobble of worry came back.

"Oh, Pandarina, it's no good. I can't dance in front of Queen Elsie. I just know I'll make a mistake."

Pandarina smiled and took Skye's hand in her soft rainbow paw. Skye felt herself growing brave. "OK, Pandarina," she smiled. "Let's do this **together**."

As the music started, the class got into position.

Princess Skye danced across
the stage with Pandarina right by her side.
She skipped, shimmied, leapt, twirled, and . . .

. . . tripped!

Skye shut her eyes tight.
She was so embarrassed!

But then she felt Pandarina's soft paw on her shoulder. Opening her eyes, she saw Queen Elsie looking straight at her, smiling a great big smile!

Pandarina took Skye's hand, and together they
kept on dancing, twirling, and whirling across the stage.

After the performance,
Queen Elsie thanked each of the
dancers. "You were wonderful,
Princess Skye," she said.

"But I tripped!" Skye blushed.

"That doesn't matter," laughed
the queen. "You got back up and
kept going! And that's the
most important thing."

With Pandarina's help, Skye had completely let go of her worries. She felt very proud of herself. Because when you try your best and have fun, you'll always be the star of the show.